Sweet dreams, Jack-Jack.

# Sweet Dreams, Jack-Jack

Inspired by

Disney · PIXAR
INCREDIBLES 2

Written by

MEREDITH RUSU

Illustrated by

GURIHIRU

DISNEP PRESS

LOS ANGELES • NEW YORK

For Mom, Dad, Andrew, and Jenny.
You will always be my Incredibles.—MR

Design by Winnie Ho

Printed in the United States of America

First Hardcover Edition, May 2018    10 9 8 7 6 5 4 3 2 1

ISBN 978-1-368-01193-8

Library of Congress Control Number: 2017961266

FAC-034274-18075

For more Disney Press fun, visit www.disneybooks.com

# This is Jack-Jack.

He's a baby just like any other.

Except his family has *Super* powers.

His dad can
lift superheavy things.

His mom can stretch superlong.

His sister can
make super force fields,
and his brother can
run superfast.

Together, they're the Incredibles!

Jack-Jack doesn't have powers. . . .

Or does he?

One night, Mr. Incredible put Jack-Jack to bed.
He read him a story.

*"In the country of Nodoff,
the Frubbers of Freep are
all giving in to the sweet
succor of sleep."*

Closed went the book. Out went the light.

And Jack-Jack went to sleep.

**Sweet dreams, Jack-Jack.**

Mr. Incredible tiptoed downstairs.
But a little while later, he heard something strange.

# Jack-Jack was out of his crib!

How did that happen?

Back upstairs they went.
Mr. Incredible read the story again.

*"All over Doozle-Dorf,*
*the Fribbers of Frupp*
*are going to sleep 'cause*
*they just can't keep up."*

Closed went the book. Out went the light.

And Jack-Jack went to sleep once more.
**Sweet dreams, Jack-Jack.**

Mr. Incredible tiptoed downstairs.

But what was this?

Jack-Jack was on the sofa watching television!

Back upstairs they went.

Mr. Incredible read the story one more time.

*"All over Doozle-Dorf, they're hitting the sack. Everyone's getting the sleep that they lack."*

Closed went the book. Out went the light.
And this time, Mr. Incredible made sure Jack-Jack
couldn't escape from his crib.

Sweet dreams,
Jack-Jack.

Mr. Incredible tiptoed downstairs. He held his breath.

He turned the corner. . . .

And there was Jack-Jack. Watching television. Again.

Oh, well. If Mr. Incredible couldn't keep Jack-Jack in his crib, they might as well watch television together.

They snuggled up on the sofa.
Soon Mr. Incredible was fast asleep.

Jack-Jack was *not* asleep. He was watching a movie
about a masked criminal robbing a jewelry store.

Suddenly, Jack-Jack heard a noise!

A raccoon was rummaging through the trash can outside.

Jack-Jack looked at the masked robber on the television.

He looked at the raccoon.

He knew what he had to do.

Jack-Jack headed to the door . . .
and passed right through!

He threw the garbage back into the trash can and closed
the lid . . . with just a look!

Jack-Jack was going to stop that raccoon robber.

He fended off the raccoon.

The raccoon fought back.

Then Jack-Jack
got all fired up!

AHRRRRR!

Now the raccoon was angry.
He put out Jack-Jack's fire.
The raccoon was certain
he'd gotten away with his
evil plan to raid the trash.

HEE, HEE, HEE.

But he was wrong!

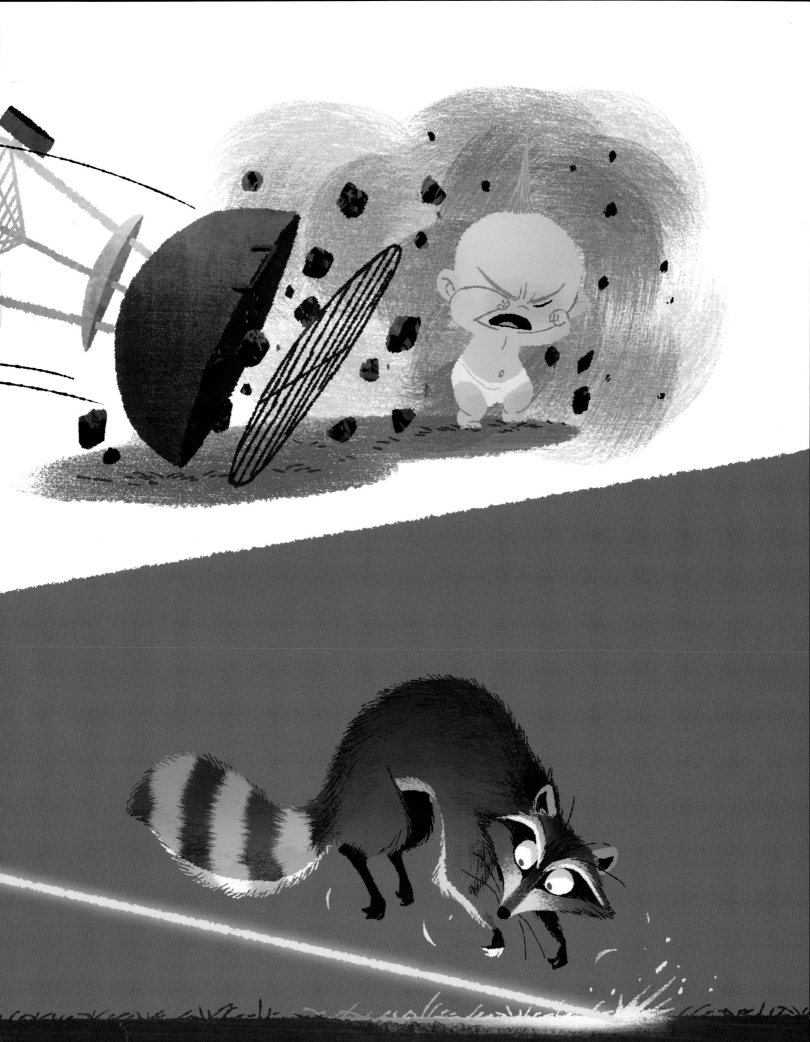

Meanwhile, all the noise had woken up
Mr. Incredible. He came out just in time to see
Jack-Jack multiply . . . into a bunch of little Jack-Jacks!

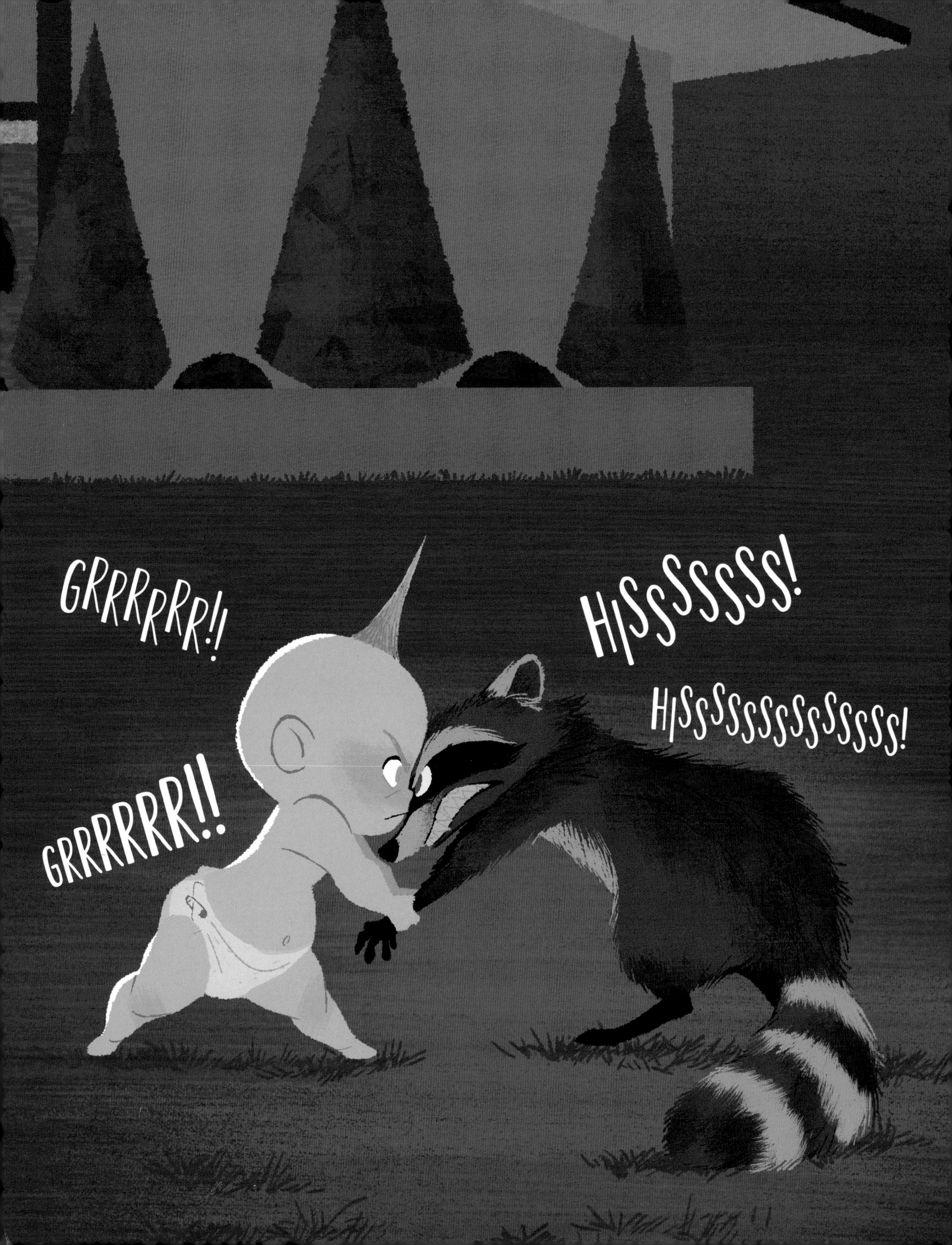
GRRRRRR!!
GRRRRRR!!
HISSSSSSS!
HISSSSSSSSSSSSSS!

The raccoon was surrounded! That was finally enough to scare the sneaky bandit away.

Mr. Incredible scooped up all the Jack-Jacks. They combined back into one sweet little baby.

"Jack-Jack, did you go through a locked door?"
Mr. Incredible asked in amazement. "And you
multiplied? You have powers! Aw, yeah!"
He rubbed noses with Jack-Jack.
**"You're a Super baby."**

Then Mr. Incredible stopped smiling.
"You're a Super baby . . . who can
multiply like rabbits . . . and pass through
any solid surface.
"Oh, no.
"What are we going to tell Mommy?"
Jack-Jack giggled.
"Let's wait until morning."